ELMO'S
Tricky Tongue Twisters

Are your lips all loose and limber?
Is your tongue tuned up and tough?
Because Elmo hopes you're ready now
To say some silly stuff!

BY SARAH ALBEE
ILLUSTRATED BY MAGGIE SWANSON

Featuring Jim Henson's Sesame Street Muppets

 A GOLDEN BOOK • NEW YORK

Published by Golden Books Publishing Company, Inc., in cooperation with Children's Television Workshop

A portion of the money you pay for this book goes to Children's Television Workshop.
It is put right back into SESAME STREET and other CTW educational projects. Thanks for helping!

Grover gobbles grapes as he gazes at gray geese in the green grass.

Selling seashells by the seashore, Snuffy got stuck in his seashell shop.

Baker Betty Lou bought some butter,
But it made her batter bitter.
So Baker Betty Lou bought some better butter
To make her bitter batter better.

Farley flips five fine flapjacks.

Mumford's in a fix doing tricks with
six silly sticks.

Big Bird wants to teach Bert to begin
to toboggan.
But the toboggan Big Bird brought Bert
is too big.

Twelve Twiddlebugs twirl
twelve twisted twigs.

Elmo sits serenely and soaks in sweet-smelling soapsuds.

Mushy bananas!
To munch the bunch would be too
much lunch.
Do you munch much mush for lunch?

Herry carried cherished chairs very
carefully down the stairs.

Oscar makes noise that annoys the
boisterous oysters.

Hoots tried to tutor two tooters
To toot on a sax and a flute.
The two tooters asked Hoots,
"Is it harder to toot or
To tutor two tooters to toot?"

Ernie can't avert squirting Bert's shirt
with dessert.

Monster sisters insist on twisting.
Hope those sisters don't get blisters.

Sherry sure hopes she'll see the sun shine soon.

Did you like this silly book?
Then have some fellow tell it again while
Elmo plays cello for some swell, bellowing
yellow elephants.